VIC CITY EXPRESS

VIC CITY EXPRESS

Yannis Tsirbas

Translated from the Greek by Fred A. Reed

Baraka
Books

Montréal

Translation © Fred A. Reed

Copyright © Yannis Tsirbas and Neveli editions 2013; in accordance with Iris Literary Agency, irislit@otenet.gr.

ISBN 978-1-77186-148-9 pbk; 978-1-77186-159-5 epub; 978-1-77186-160-1 pdf; 978-1-77186-161-8 mobi/pocket

Book Design by Folio infographie
Cover illustration: Vincent Partel

Editing and proofreading: Robin Philpot & David Warriner

Legal Deposit, 3rd quarter 2018
Bibliothèque et Archives nationales du Québec
Library and Archives Canada

Published by Baraka Books of Montreal
6977, rue Lacroix
Montréal, Québec H4E 2V4
Telephone: 514 808-8504
info@barakabooks.com

Trade Distribution & Returns
Canada and the United States
Independent Publishers Group
1-800-888-4741 (IPG1);
orders@ipgbook.com

Printed and bound in Quebec

We acknowledge the support from the Société de développement des entreprises culturelles (SODEC), the Government of Quebec tax credit for book publishing administered by SODEC and the Government of Canada.

Société
de développement
des entreprises
culturelles
Québec

Funded by the Government of Canada
Financé par le gouvernement du Canada

Canada

*"There is no such thing as an empty chair;
someone must always get up
in order for you to sit down."*

Louis Althusser

"Okay pal, let's take it from the top. Sixth: old lady Alithinou, all by her lonesome up there in the penthouse. 1-0. Fifth: the Albanians in the double. Two parents, two kids, 1-4. And in the triple, the Loukas family. Pensioners both. Never know if they're alive or dead. That makes 3-4. Fourth, the Kourtises with their kids; four of 'em all together, nice people, like the Albanians; an old lady, a couple with their kid, four altogether. What does that give us? 6-7? Down one on three; us and Alexandr the tile-man. Ukrainian, unmarried. 11-9. From then on you lose count. Next floor down, seven or eight Bangladeshis at least, ugly little buggers, in the three-room. Don't have a clue what they cook in there but ever since they moved in the whole building stinks of onions. Them plus two old East European ladies in the double. In their sixties, quiet, clean; don't get me wrong, must've been good looking back when. 11-19 and counting. Next floor down comes the Santo Domingo annex. Rachel, professional streetwalker, her daughter—husband unknown—about fourteen, tall, you should see her boobs; who's the father? Not a clue. Plus the daughter's daughter, father unknown of course, still in the stroller, plus the grandmother. A whorehouse you say? The customers don't count of course. Bound to be some Greeks too. People coming and going, day and night. Next door old lady Kalatzis. Can't hear, can't see; when she watches TV she plasters her mug up against the screen. When I was a kid she'd look after me, wash my hands in the bathtub, now she's stone deaf. Final score: 12 to 24. A double. Add the old lady's housekeeper; Bulgarian or something like that and we're up to 12 to 25! What can you do? At first it didn't bother me personally; I was used to it, if you know what I mean. Yeah, terrific! These days you go for a stroll down by the Museum and right there, at the main entrance, they're snorting shit. Not outside, on Averoff Street. No. Inside, right behind the columns. The National Museum of shit. That's where I live, pal."

I look out the window as the trees rush by at high speed in perfect file. The guy keeps on talking.

"That's not all pal; I step outside and there's Pakistanis selling stuff piled up on sheets right there, on the ground. Undershorts, socks, undershirts, gloves, caps. Fish even. They dump some funny-looking fish on top of cardboard boxes and sell 'em. No ice, I tell you; zilch. One big stink. Another guy, bananas. Bread by the sackful. I take the other sidewalk, the one along Acharnon Street on my way to work and it's like I'm skiing in some slalom race. Got to walk in the street where maybe I get clipped by a car. Then there's the barbershops. Always getting their hair cut, these guys. Morning to night they're open; people lined up outside. Barbershops with Arabic signs every block. How come they're always getting their hair cut? Beats me. It says so in the Koran?"

I shake my head. No idea. Where does he get his hair cut, I ask him?

"At Mary's, pal, on Alcibiades Street. Since I was twelve. Used to be over on Heyden, in a half-basement. Only charges me eight euros. Normally it's twelve. She knows me since I was a kid. Okay, I don't have a hell of a lot of hair, so she gives me a discount."

He laughs at his own joke. I smile.

"Further along, up until Epirus Street, you got the Romanian travel agencies. Athens-Bucharest fifty euros, pre-crisis, that is. After, forty. You know how the Albanians are, a bit farther along, next to the railway tracks, before you get to Karaïskakis Square? Well, here the Romanians have it all to themselves. At first there was only Lilian Travel, then came Perla, and now there's Murat Tours too. A Romanian travel agency every thirty-forty yards. Bigger demand. Fridays and Saturdays, no way you can get through. I go to get the car from the garage; all hell is breaking loose. They leave Fridays, Saturdays for up north and there's a line-up of busses with baggage racks and people swarming in all directions. Everywhere Romanians with their suitcases and those plastic fake travel bags of theirs, cramming into the busses. Can't move an inch what with the Chinamen hawking all kinds of crap as they climb on board. Then off they go."

Do you walk to work? I ask. I glance out the window hoping to figure out just where we are. I can feel the train gaining speed.

"Yeah, when I've got work. I can't take the metro, or the trolley bus. You grab a strap and it sticks to your hand. Plus I don't have to pay fare. I turn at the corner of Epirus and Acharnon. Just across the street from Murat's travel agency; there's this Chink who sells clothes, monkey shoes crap like that. Belts, glasses. Just up from his place and all along Epirus is where the Africans hang out. Night and day. You know how they do it? Sleep in shifts. Forty winks in rotation, pal. Twenty of 'em rent a flat no way they can all cram in there to sleep. So while you're asleep I'm like strolling up and down on Acharnon and Epirus, waiting for my turn. Men and women all together, with their kids tied onto their backs. The other guys, the ones with the barbershops, men; their women? Out of sight."

On he drones. I'm getting bored so I glance at the incoming emails on my cell. Nothing but spam. | Asvestolakos Restaurant | Pet Badges | HIV-Hepatitis B tests! Cheap! | Full-body massage | Who buys discount hepatitis tests anyway?

"The square, that's the heartbreaker. Nothing like it at St. Panteleimon's that they're always talking about on TV, or anywhere else. Take a stroll any time you like over to the church; nobody will lay a hand on you. All the rest, bullshit. It's bright, it's clean; kiosks open day and night. Just because they closed the playground? Big deal. We used to make fun of the kids who lived around the church. They were the proles in the neighborhood, buddy. At school we came from three spots: Attica, Victoria and St. Panteleimon's.

The kids from there were number two's, by a long shot. Like, white socks and all the rest, if you get my meaning. We'd fight and fight some more. The numbskulls, they all came from there. Had the worst snack bars. Me, I live two lights down the street from the church and one from the square. We'd only go there to shoot some pool, to the Billiard Academy on Acharnon, in a half-basement. But what really bugs me, pal, is the square."

Which one is that? I ask him offhand.

"Vic City, kiddo! You know, the Victoria subway station. Nobody could get us out of there. And now you don't even dare walk by outside. They'll close down the street and fight it out. One race against the other. Some of 'em fell down and guys were kicking them while they lay there on the street. Traffic was blocked. Like, it was blood on the sidewalks."

I look him over and can't resist the impulse to egg him on. I keep listening to his voice over the monotonous clicking of the train.

"And does it ever stink, pal! Hash and piss. They toke up, if you get my meaning, all along Heyden in the old buildings just before Filis Street you get high just walking by. They take a drag and then cut a slash right there on the sidewalk. Snort; then piss it off. Moroccans, Algerians, people like that. They're the ones with the dope; grows wild down there. And the exact spot the Algerian was pissing the night before the Pakistani lays out his bed sheet and sells underwear the next day; see what I mean?"

Does he really need to go by that way, I ask him. Just asking. I delete the next email. | Foot massage | Weight loss – detox | Professional Extermination | Water heater service | Firm up your buttocks |

"From there I hit the video club, and then I'll drop off at a café in the square, buy me a sandwich. Those guys, though, they're all looking for a fight, you can tell. One gang here, another gang there. Nothing but bone and muscle, skinny, dark, like Rafik Djebbour, you know who I'm talking about, right, the soccer player? You get the picture; whole gangs of Djebbours standing around, snorting dope and pissing and you're trying to make your way through 'em carrying your shopping bag from the video club. They'll try to grab whatever you've got; no surprise there. Cellphones, purses, you hear all kinds of stories. When they're not fighting among themselves that is. Let 'em spot a woman alone and there's trouble. They ain't getting nothing; no woman will look at 'em. Underdeveloped guys, panting, tongues always hanging out. If I decide to go another way around I have to take one of the side streets off Filis. No way you can get around the stink of piss, but down there it's dark, not a soul; just as likely you'll get mugged. Grab your flip-flops, undershorts even. That's the way it always was. Hell, when we were kids in the back alleys we'd get whatever we could. There'd be ten-twelve of us; we'd come across some guy doing the rounds of the cathouses and we'd jump him. Grab his jacket, Unlimited was the style back then, you know, the stuffed ones. Goosies we called 'em. Boots too. Doc Martens. Know how many of those guys walked away barefoot? Just give us the socks and money, if you get my meaning. High-school kids we were. Eighty-eight, eighty-nine, we're talking. Me, a gang from Saint Paul's got me. Down the hill, next to the basketball court. Hit me for ten thousand drachs. They didn't give shit about my clothes. I wasn't into brand names anyway; no cash to spare in our family. Ten thousand; that was big money back then. Didn't touch me; I handed it right over. Only as I was leaving one of 'em grabs a sack of garbage from a trashcan and dumps it over my head. Just like that, for the hell of it. I wipe off my face; got off easy I figure. Later, when I was with the guys I tried to spot 'em; no way."

When did things change? I ask him.

"Listen pal, beats me. Like one minute it wasn't and the next minute it was. We started hearing about it on TV, in the papers and so on. You were ashamed to say where you lived. Especially at St. Panteleimon's. The first one was this guy, Pantelis and his kids, from southern Albania and a couple or three Pollaks you'd smell the beer on 'em when you met 'em in the elevator. Warzycha and Wandzik, that's all they cared about. Champions' League; those were the years. Back then. Green and White fans, all of 'em. Not one Ukrainian. Back then. After the match they'd fight it out on the stairs with beer bottles. Broken Amstel bottles. They only drank Amstel, Easties we called 'em. Later came the others. Get the picture? Now the Albanians are pulling out, one after the other. Moving up. That leaves us, stuck with the dregs. One day I'm in Vic City and I look around me. Swarming with people, hundreds of 'em. Easties, 'Roccans, Pakis, you name it, we got it. Pushing and shoving; like in some cheap club. Kids playing in the dirt, the statue full of Arabic letters in red spray. What do they say? Go figure. Dogs, women in headscarves; people going every which way; garbage all over the place! When did it happen? I don't know, but it was, like, you go to sleep and it's not there and you wake up the next morning and here's this mess, pal."

Now he wants to describe the square.

"At the head of September Third Street there used to be a fountain. After school we'd have water fights. On the bottom there were colored lights, under water; don't touch 'em they said, you'll get an electric shock. Red ones, blue ones. At some point they tore it down. Can't remember when. In the middle was the statue. The one that was in Constitution Square before. So they told the Citizens' Committee. Theseus it was, I think. Can't remember. Or maybe some goddess. Covered with shit, pigeon shit. Like in the song 'There was this statue that saw me...' It was Lefteris Papadopoulos who wrote it, yeah, him. Used to be my neighbor, can you believe it? Went to Public School just around the corner. Villa Amalia it was. Amalia who? I say. Acharnon and Heyden."

Gotcha

ACHARNON AND HEYDEN; at the corner.
Second Boys Gymnasium. Were you a tough
kid or weren't you? Junta times. One day this
patrol car pulls up outside. Dome light on
top like a big fat pimple full of blue pus. The
cops pile out, just doing their job. They don't
lock the doors. Who's going to mess with
them? You're a tough kid, right? All the kids
scared of you. Wanted to hang out with you.
Not too close; not too far. Almost never had
to hit them. No need. You'd grab their nose

with your fingers like a pair of pliers; twist 'til they cried. Really hurts. You feel it once, you know what it's like. Yours got busted in gym class when you were twelve. Didn't have to do it; but you did. Recess time. You can drive, Meleti? Sure you can. With one leap you clear the fence, open the driver's door looking over your shoulder; make sure everyone's watching. Turn the key in the ignition. Rev it a couple of times to clear the exhaust and tear off, laying rubber. You turn on the dome light, siren full blast. Turn right down Acharnon, take a right on Derigny, right again on Filis, another right on Heyden and end up with a fishtail in front of the school. Once around the block. Everybody's lined up at the fence watching. It's you they're watching. Not a sound. The janitor rings the bell, back to class he yells. Nobody budges. Everybody wants to see the tough guy. You get out of the car, hands in the air. Clapping and whistling; the siren still shrieking its head off. The neighbors were watching from their balconies. The tough guy, that's who you were.

They whip the piss out of you. Two days they hold you at the station and beat you. Fifteen years old you were; they work you over but good. Finally your dad calls a friend of his and they let you go. It helped you were a minor. Dad was a right-winger; your boxing coach put in a good word for you.

You went back to school. Lips all puffed up; didn't feel a thing, black eyes, hunched over a bit; your ribs hurt. Didn't matter, it wasn't the first time. You were the tough kid. The guard took one look at you and let you in. Well now, here's Meleti the chauffeur. Nice mug you've got there, Meleti. Like a roasted eggplant, kiddo. You waved your fist under his nose.

Your pride was like a fever. Sure they worked you over. You were the one. Now nobody would come near you. The kid next to you—Moustroufos was his name—switched desks. The rest sat three to a desk and there you were, all by yourself. From the teachers not a peep. That's what really hurt: more than anything else. For nothing they made you look bad. Nobody was going to spit on you. Just because of the cops? Only one thing they understood, you thought. That afternoon after school you waited for your desk mate down at the corner, in front of his house. He saw you standing there; he knew. Dropped his school bag; didn't let out a sound. You beat him until he spat out two teeth on the sidewalk. You didn't say a word. Next day he sat down right beside you. Everybody saw him; got the message. But you wanted more. That's who you were.

You heard about a guy a few blocks over who did tattoos. You looked him up. Tattoo me, you said. Get out of here you little shit, he said. You showed him your fist. Those were the days when you made mistakes. The days when all you could do was make mistakes. Okay, kid, he said. Where do you want it? Right here, down low. Where down low, kid? My prick. Get out of here, you punk. Show me how to do it and I'll do it myself. What should it say, the jerk asks. APEX. What's that? You know, "Greek Police" I say. The guy couldn't stop laughing. It hurt bad but you didn't make a sound. Blood on your undershorts for days.

You showed it to a few guys in the can. That did it. Tough guy. No secret. Everybody in Vic City knew about Meleti and his tattoo. The cops too, they found out soon enough. Nabbed you again. Found you at Mimi's billiard hall on Aristotle Street. Easy; everybody hung out there.

Two days they worked you over. Again. But only kicks. And only down there, down low. Stripped you, four of 'em; pinned you down so you couldn't move while the fifth guy kicked you. Domazos, Antoniadis, they shoot they score! Domazos, Antoniadis, they shoot they score. The cop was laughing. Domazos, you knew about him. Had a shop on the square; plates and glasses, stuff like that; your mom would buy things there. Wembley Stadium, seventy-one it was, the European Cup final; Vic City was where they really went wild; people all the way from here to Omonia Square, downtown. Thousands on September Third Street. While they were kicking you, you remembered your mom. The way her homespun apron smelled. Food and bleach. Another cop—just for variety— would poke it with the tip of his shoe and grind it on the floor. I'll rub it out you little shit, he yelled; flatten it out like a cigarette butt.

Months you pissed blood. Tried to get something going on your own; maybe you could get it to work. Went to a whore. She laughed. Kid, maybe you want it, but nothing's gonna happen. Punched her out. Felt her nose break. You could tell when your fist cracked the bone. She didn't want any money; only for you to get out. But you paid her: fair and square. After, your dad dragged you to a doctor. With you he was joking. Hey, Meleti; a little thing like that bothers a boxer like you? But he took your father aside. You knew.

The cops came calling again. This time they wanted some info. About a student at school; they had suspicions. With the first kick down there, low, you sang. Started to cry. Not that, guys. Don't make me stool. After, you fingered another guy, and another. They even paid you off.

Now you're fifty-three, kneeling on your bed. Sweat dripping into your eyes. Through the balcony door you can see your old school; it's a ruin now, with a torn banner hanging from the roof that says "occupation." Corner of Heyden and Acharnon. You're stuck here. Never left your four walls. Alexandra Boulevard on the right; St. Meletios Street on the left; farther down, Liosion and over one, Patission: the four outer limits of your life. Georgi fucking you from behind. He's good. Strong; lasts and lasts. Big tool. You met him one night, grabbed him by the nose until he dropped to his knees and begged you to let up, some shit bar on Ithaca Street it was where you were working as a bouncer; him, he was trying to impress the girls. Back and forth you're going, whole body shaking. Georgi's got a real hard-on today. Smacks your ass. It hurts, you think of other things. Take it easy sweetie, you say. Ease off. Georgi shoots off inside you and after, kisses you on the neck. You turn over and light a cigarette. You take a fifty-euro bill from the dresser and hand it to him.

I love you so much sweetie, he says as he sticks the fifty between his teeth and zips up his jeans. You watch the smoke float up toward the light and hang from the ceiling.

You jump to your feet and catch Georgi at the door. Already I miss you, you say and softly you take his nose between your first and second fingers.

"Gotcha," you say.

* * *

He rattles on, unstoppable. And as he does I delete the incoming garbage from my cell. | Wedding photography | Peeling set | Speed Dating Exclusive | Springtime allergy test | Unique Design Water Bottle |

"Our statue's one big pile of bird shit and writing nobody can read. The mulberry trees, that's where it's at, pal. Two rows on each side of the square two, three meters apart. Imagine, natural goalposts. No need to put down some rocks; nothing. We'd play soccer like with real goals whole tree trunks for goalposts. So our ball was a flattened Coca-Cola bottle cap, big shit. But those goalposts, they were for real. You tell me, what other square you could score a top corner goal in? And up from the fountain, at the subway entrance, tables everywhere. Coffee shops. My first coffee. Savoy, Maxim's. Today the Savoy is The Palms, and Maxim's is a fast-food joint. There was a pastry shop at the corner; closed too. The fast food joints pal, if you need to take a leak you've got to buy something and they give you a code for the toilets along with your receipt. To pee you need a PIN, get it? 'Cause everybody wants to pee and shit for free so they had to put passwords on the WC. You want to take a shit, they're telling you, gotta buy a cheeseburger. So you go and you shit on the grass. Where you gonna shit if you don't have a home to go to, forget a two-spot for a cheeseburger? Got rid of the tables too. To clean up the square they said. So now you've got the blacks with their CDs and their belts and their handbags. You get off the subway and you fall all over them."

"What's on the other side?"

"Down towards Aristotle Street is the worst. One day a drag queen wagging his ass comes down to Vic City on his way back from some shopping trip for sure, and there was this gang of Georgians hanging around. Tough people, Christians. They began to taunt the fag. But he stood up to them; wasn't going to take it. So they stomped him. Shopping bags this way, provisions that

way; they busted his ribs. I heard he's looking to move out. There used to be swings
down there; all gone now. A teeter-totter in
a sand pit and a slide. Nothing but concrete
now. That's where the Pat-Cute grill was,
and just across from it was Krouskas, now
that was a snack bar. You could smell the
meatballs and the fries as you walked by.
Those were sandwiches! You'd swear you
were at the soccer pitch. Couldn't wait to
grab a big bite. Upstairs from Pat-Cute was
the Stratigakis Preparatory Academy. A nice
neoclassic building it was. Didn't last long.
Pat-Cute closed too. Nothing left. When
you get right down to it, the funny thing is
when a place doesn't close, not that it closes.
Listen buddy, I'm watching TV and I see guys
smiling, or even someone who doesn't look
like he's got a worry in the world and I look
him over and I ask myself if the guy's really
got any bread. How do they do it? Do they

work, regular jobs, dough from their folks, maybe they're broke and just pretending to be in the money? Go figure. I'm the only one who can't sleep at night? I'm the only one who's worried, pal, about my mom and my dad and they can't make ends meet?"

Does he live alone or with them I ask. Clearly, he doesn't want to dwell on the subject.

"With the old folks, buddy. Then, like I was saying, there's the kiosks. The one at the top of the square, that's where they knew us all by our first names; we'd hang out there, but there was no swiping. From the next one over, where Sammy our classmate worked, you grabbed anything you could. Once he put modeling clay in his ears and blocked 'em. We're talking grade school. It was all the teacher could do to get it out. The whole day, up in smoke. See, he operated a kiosk, his folks that is, but he ran the place since high school. We'd go buy something, a package of gum for instance; one of us would keep Sammy busy while the others would grab whatever they could, magazines, candies, you know *Serafino, Tiramola,* crap like that. One of my classmates, a guy named Roussos, we asked him 'how much,' five fingers he said, meaning 'nothing.' He stole it right under the guy's eyes. Gave him the money and when he took the change he'd grab a piece of gum, Bubbalou it was. That kiosk was the crappiest; empty shelves, not much merchandise, dirty. Later an Albanian bought it, ran it into the ground and now it opens one day, closes the next. We didn't bother with the kiosks farther down, only if the upper ones ran out of something. Saw Sammy years later on the street, part-time worker at some theater over in Kypseli, moving, setting up and taking down, stuff like that."

Am I listening he asks. Yes, I'm listening.

"Like I was saying, I hike up to Kolonaki where the big shots live. Can you tell me, pal, why they pick up garbage three times a day there, but for us, only once a week...if we're lucky? What would you call that? Some new world order kind of thing? Now and then there's no pick-up at all. Their trash is better than ours? They've got priority? If you head up along Academy Street, it gets better; leave Patissia behind and things change. One block at a time. First it's dark but later it gets brighter as you go up. As if we're some kind of plebs. As clear as day, pal. Don't get me started about University Avenue. Lit up bright as day. Okay, not all the way. Handout artists; blacks with their sheets on the sidewalk. Umbrellas when it rains. But up there they chase 'em away. Real long-distance champs, they are. But for us, well, we're on our own."

I turn my head toward the window and stop listening. He's still talking I imagine. The window feels cool on my forehead. We enter a tunnel, and the darkness relieves my eyes. All of a sudden he starts up again, just as I thought he'd fallen asleep.

"...shopping carts, pal. Know what I mean? Whole families pushing 'em down the street. Wherever you turn. Everybody's got his shopping cart. Mom and dad digging through the garbage while the kids push the cart. The little ones just sitting there, alongside the trash. A lot of them stick the kids in the bins. The ones that don't have a hook. Grab 'em by the waist and hold 'em upside down while they rummage around looking for something to eat. Sometimes you see 'em jumping up and down in there. They fix special tools, I'm telling you. Hooks with long handles. Organized! Metal; aluminum, stainless steel is what they're looking for. They sell it. Like

I said, you go out to work in the morning and you're afraid a cart will run over you, along with everything else."

Well, we've got our own scavengers, I say, as if all of a sudden it was like I wanted to be a full participant in the discussion. Beggars too. Been around for a long time. No sooner did I say it than it seemed to have been a ridiculous thing to say; too late, I couldn't take it back. Don't know why I said it. I stop, as if someone was listening. Awkwardly I glance at my telephone screen.

Happiness is a sandwich

THREE DAYS. Since I ate. Three days. A cheese sandwich missing a bite. Some kid dropped it. Bang, a slap from his mom. And into the garbage. I fished it out. Ate it. Three days. A cheese sandwich. Head spinning. One step forward. Stop. Two steps; stop again. I'm at the square. Hungry. Thirsty. Fountain. Water. I ask for money. Stretch out my hand. Ten drachmas. Twenty. Nobody gives if you're young. Dizzy. I remember what food was like. Hunger is like a dream. Taste the food.

Fill my belly. Belch. Stomach hurts. Empty. Everything a blur.

I sit down at the edge of the fountain. Lean over to drink. Head spinning. I fall into the water. I'm soaked. Just want to get out of here. Everybody's looking. Shame. My shoes, heavy. Squish. Water runs down my body. Now I'm shivering. Everybody can hear me. No way I can be alone. Everybody's watching. Dizzy. Head spinning. Cold. Some kids go by. Laughing. I look down. Ground revolving. Feel the water running down my body down onto my feet. Dripping off me.

Right in front of me I see a scrap of paper. Blue. Has number five on it. Head spinning. Plus three zeros. Five thousand drachs! Now what do I do? Three steps. One step forward. My shoes squish. The five thou bill, it's spinning. As if it wants to get away. Another step. A breath of wind. I shiver. One more step and I'll eat my fill. Finally some food. Just a little this way. Crisp. A breath of wind will take it away. Another step. I bend over. Almost crawling. I slip. Dizzy. I go down. I burst on the cement like a water-filled balloon. Don't have the strength to get up. Can't see the money. It was an illusion.

I'm face down on the paving stones of the square. I see them close up. Little furrows. Furrows in my stomach. I'm hungry. Don't feel a thing. When you're that hungry nothing exists. You don't feel a thing. The five thou bill, that's all I remember. Warm pavement. Warms my hands. Relief. I'm soaked. I feel all around me. Slap my hands on the cement. As hard as I can. I'm like a baby I think. Money nowhere. Only in my head. Got to get up. No regrets. Only hunger. I'm heavy now. Starving and yet so heavy? I brace myself to get up. Can feel paper on one hand. The fiver is stuck to my hand. Already I've had my fill!

Now I've got a good grip on it. Standing no problem, I got wings; now I'm crossing the square, dragging my feet but moving fast; past the fountain, a fast-food joint just across the way, splat, I go in, dripping; I see myself in the window, water dripping from my hair, drops on my lips or maybe I'm drooling; even the smell makes me happy, the crowd in the stands, my father; happiness is a sandwich; I order a double cheese with bacon, meatballs, smoked meat, ham, mushrooms, roasted pepper, tomato and mayonnaise. Go pay first the guy tells me; I go. What? They don't change big fives. Please, I'm hungry I say. That's the way it is, he says. Go change it. Where? I can't hold on much longer. I'm dripping water all over the place, he says. Get out. I'll change it and come back. Where? What about the sandwich? First make change, he says.

Head spinning. The whole square, spinning. Can you make change for me? Nobody answers. People turn away. The fountain; it's spinning too. Just want to sit down. Can you make change for me? It's counterfeit I hear. I sit down. Can you make change? Nobody. I go over to the kiosk. Can you change this for me? He takes it. Like he's stroking it between his fingers. Where'd you find it? Hands it back. I stroke it, with two fingers. Just like him. Not perfectly smooth. Soothes my fingertips. My legs won't carry me much farther. Can you change this for me? Hungry. Dizzy. Can you make change? Squish, squash. I'm delirious now. Shouting. Make change for me? I'm waving the crisp big five now. My legs won't hold me. I sit down on the edge of the fountain. A kid is running this way and that through the pigeons. They take to the air. Heading straight for me. Behind him his mom is trying to catch up. Right in my direction. Good looking. I can barely make her out. He takes the money from my hand. I let it go. Got no strength. He's got a piece of candy in his hand; half-melted. He holds it out in my direction. Good kid. Now his mom has just about caught up with him. Don't! she yells at the kid. I grab the candy and stuff it into my mouth. With the wrapper. She grabs the bill from her son. What did I tell you? She tears it up and throws the pieces into the air. I belch.

* * *

| How to eat your fill during Lent | Let our clowns entertain your kids | We train your dog | Music lessons | Say goodbye to cellulite |

"What's the connection anyway, pal? Sure we've got scavengers. Like that's some big deal? Something to brag about? What's the connection? What are you trying to say, anyway?"

It's getting dark. The sky is turning deep purple and orange. Spring can't be far away. I decide to pop the question. Would he ever do anything—you know—violent?

"Would I ever? Would. I. Ever."

He laughs, a bit forced. Quickly turns serious; looks me in the eye.

"We'll start with bread. Me, I've got this idea. It'll be an epidemic. Everybody will be doing the same thing, like an epidemic. Our leftovers and mostly bread, we'll put 'em in separate bags and leave 'em next to the bins. So people can find 'em. So people can eat."

I don't get what he's saying. He says the last words in a kind of drawl. Sarcastically. Then he turns his head and says, in a low voice, "people."

Laughs. More like a snigger. And shuts his eyes. Now he'll doze off, I say to myself. With one hand he shifts his head around, can't get comfortable. Then goes on, a bit irritated.

"Where did you say you live, pal?"

Grew up in St. Paraskevi, I say.

"Posh digs."

He puckers his lips.

"How would you like it if every day a truck full of chickens parked in front of your house? Every afternoon around four, let's say. Right at the corner of Acharnon. One big cage full of chickens; live chickens. The Pakis, the Afghans and all the others are milling around, buying a live chicken. And after, off they go in every direction, chicken in hand. You call this the twenty-first century? You call this the capital city? And where are they going? Back to their flats, that's where. And me, who lives next to some Paki with his chicken like it's back in 1950, pal; what are we anyway, some chicken coop? I mean, how would you like to live in this neighborhood, my fine gentleman?

Let me tell you! You go out for a stroll in the district where you grew up, pal, like where I grew up, and there's this Paki heading for you carrying a live chicken by the feet and the bird is screeching its head off and in the other hand he's got this transistor radio blasting oriental music. 'Cause we're stuck with that too; the transistors. And whoever doesn't have one is walking around with a cell playing the United Arab Emirates' top ten, just to give you some idea."

He waves his hand up and down excitedly. I catch myself looking toward the other passengers to see if there's anyone who could help should the need arise.

"Well, one time I just lost it, pal. There I was in the car, on Acharnon Street, just in front of my old high school, the one that's gone full out multicultural. That's what they throw in our faces; that's why everything's going to hell. Multiculturalism, globalization they call it; enough already. So I'm out of gas and there I am, humiliated at the gas station; 'five euros' I tell the attendant. Five euros worth of gas, pal; did you ever pump five euros worth of gas? No sooner does he start than he pulls out the nozzle. So right in front of me, at the stop light, there's this guy crossing the street, you know, in front of the Masonic lodge, the one with the gilded doors and the square and compass above, the nicest building anywhere around. So, ambling across the street comes this darkie with an ice-cream cone in his hand, full up and overflowing with chocolate syrup and chopped nuts and whatever else they put. Get a load of this, I say. And there he is, slurping away not a worry in the world. And he's got flip-flops on and what do I see? The white bottoms of his feet and between his toes; disgusting. And me, I can't even afford gas, pal, and it's all I can do to make ends meet; one-euro smokes is all I can afford, contraband Gold Mounts, you know 'em—how would you know?—straw from some stable. In the back streets a few blocks over you can find some Armenian women, or maybe they're Kurds, holding a pack in their hand, flashing it; you hand 'em a ten-spot and they disappear into the building where they keep their stock and come out with a carton. Can't remember the last time I ate ice cream; all I can manage is the basic necessities and here's this African guy licking an ice-cream cone? This guy's got enough dough for a meal plus dessert? So me, I go nuts, pal. Nuts. On go the flashers and I climb out of the car and I go psst and with the first punch there goes the ice-cream and with the second he's on the sidewalk, one flip-flop this way, the other that way. Friend, friend, he says, talking Greek; friend my ass I go and kick him in the face, and there go his teeth, the whole works.

Another night

[...] just get me out of here the shop in Vic
City's all mine nothing missing three years
now lucky I can get ahead not curse out this
shit hole of a fabric store okay it puts bread
on my table lift this haul that my shoulders
hurt my sides carry that's all the jerk lets me
do come on pa gimme a little more nope
he says when I was your age I was grazing a
hundred sheep and two hundred goats and
whatever else I don't give a fuck pa you can
go graze three hundred camels for all I care.

[...] they call that school nothing but booze and pills you know Valium and Ativan crazy stuff cough syrup they'd dose us first thing in the morning before prayers so we could hear just fine and there was Olympia in the can sucking us off we'd tip her now and then some another slut would lick us nice and easy got out of middle school didn't crack a book then my father took over and from then on no rest.

[...] ditched the old man signed up for the army had a couple of good buddies back then there was so much drugs that we fed 'em to the dogs dissolved 'em in their water boot camp in Samos you couldn't tell the dogs from the soldier boys stoned out of their minds just like here, is what I mean.

[...] army days all we did was jerk off when I get out I meet Garyfalia the girl looks to straighten me out and she like straightens me out and she's like heaven to me the girl was and the store and the old man I could live with 'em and I stopped jerking off and now it's all gone, all the girls like Garyfalia time doesn't pass if you don't give it a shove there was a bookcase and soccer and XX movies now and then and books lots of books I liked the ones with pictures we had plenty at home, the encyclopedia with photos of statues drove me nuts you could see naked breasts medical articles that showed women's tubes and their ovaries even I still remember that book used to shoot off when I was a kid one time I soiled it and scrubbed to clean up the page and mom walks in and I shut it fast and the pages are glued together I could never get 'em open again and you couldn't see the tubes unless you held the stuck pages up to the light but she didn't say a word mom didn't the odd time I take a book or two from the bookcase Petros keeps a diary but it's all bullshit you've got to write down everything you do in the morning we wake up, roll call, eat breakfast take a shit jack off every day's gonna be the same what's all this diary crap.

[...] to make mom happy I ask her to bring me a book now and then, with pictures showing lots of people all together street demonstrations wars battles I like it when I see people all together turns me on seems right all those people in one place so many they've got to be right at least when you're there along with 'em right alongside all those people and they all agree with you and you agree with them and you know it and they know it no need to say a word now that's something.

[...] so maybe I got on her case couldn't take her chattering one time I threw a bottle of olive oil right at her it didn't miss her by much hit the kitchen wall splat a big oil stain took three days to clean up and my sister came saw her crying she cursed me and I smacked her and that's when I left that madhouse of theirs the first time.

[...] with my buddy Panayote the one they found face up one morning in Vic City from tainted shit when he died wasn't nobody to cry for him picked up some broads up in the park at Champs-de-Mars where they were building the garage for the courthouse and we go and smoke joints right there in the construction site down in the basement we're scared shitless there in the dark there are real junkies and dealers with knives they mean business hey you girls come such and such a day to this or that neoclassical building down by the Museum they tell us there's always a party and the party was totally a big joke music all goth nothing but zombies we clear out after about a half hour plus the bimbos dump us anyway.

[...] like where we gonna go now? we said school tomorrow morning but we weren't goin' home for nothing so downtown we go to catch a fuck-flick 'cause we all have hard-ons thinking we're gonna catch some real ass so we hike over to the Arion you know near the old central market down in the basement place was open 'til morning like all the skin-flick joints I'd really get it off would hit me take my breath away all I could do not to grab it then and there so I hustle into the john the one with those rotten blue wooden doors or maybe it was the Ciné Laou a few blocks over can't remember which one down I plop on the can and get pumping I'm looking around spot an eye peeking through the crack fuck this I give the door a kick pull up my shorts and go out who was it some guy looking for ass it was Panayote morning I wake up for school and run into my old man in the kitchen drinking that piss-coffee of his at least the only thing I learn from the old fart is how to make a decent Greek coffee if it's porn you want sonny boy I'll give you the money gimme a break pa you want to be all over me at the skin flicks and when I jerk off you'd be there too if you could telling me how to beat it I couldn't look him in the eye for a week he was on my case the old prick and whatever I did he was watching 'til I was seventeen at least for sure until I got myself a motorbike he was there and times I'm sure he's looking and when I lie down and forget to close my mouth so flies won't get in he humiliated me in front of everybody and now when I stare at the ceiling mouth wide open on account of the adenoids hey dad you forgot I had adenoids can't breathe right you forgot you old asshole?

[...] night time again I walk back and forth groans coming from the cells and the walls and the ceiling and the bars that pierce my guts and my head I can't take it any more.

Another night.

* * *

Now I know what the word *astonished* means. It's like everyone is listening but whenever I turn my head no one is looking at us. I could swear that all the passengers are following our conversation but as soon as I glance at them they shift their gaze at the very last minute. For the first time he turns his head, looks me straight in the eye. In that singular instant I try to understand. To understand *him*. But I see nothing in his expression, only doubt and nothing more. But doubt itself is no motive. A simple doubt can't possibly be a motive. Now I understand why I don't ask him anything really important. I don't ask because I don't know. How can you possibly explain everything that's going on? In order to understand what's happening you've got to see it on the news. Otherwise there's nothing to it. Simply doesn't exist. No other way you can get your mind around it. Someone's got to serve it up for you. But without being able to touch you, without there being the slightest possibility of human contact. I need a screen. If only there could be a screen set up between us. He's ranting. Well, not exactly ranting. I scroll down, delete all the messages. Everything obeys its own logic; I always believed that. How can I not believe it? That's who I am. I don't ask because I don't know what to expect for an answer. I never ask unless I've got some idea of what the answer will be. Should I ask how did it all get started, pal? Pal? You're talking, pal, like nothing is going on. I don't ask. Maybe I don't ask because I've got this bourgeois courtesy Vasso is always on my case about. I don't want to have strong disagreements with strangers. Not with anybody, actually. What am I supposed to say to him? Talk about democracy and violence and culture? He starts up again, in a much lower voice now, almost like a confession. He realizes he may have gone too far. But maybe it's only me thinking that.

"They eat the pigeons, you get what I'm saying? It wasn't the dogs. They ate all the pigeons. There used to be hundreds of 'em, all over the square. The whole place, swarming with pigeons. We'd put poison on the balconies, the windows, hang it from the bannisters. To keep away the lousy pigeons that shit all over the place and they eat 'em anyway. Lots of people have seen 'em going after the birds crawling in the flowerbeds, on the sidewalk, wherever they spot 'em they grab 'em for their next meal. That's where I live, pal. Where they eat pigeons and keep live chickens and buy rotten fish out of cardboard boxes like they're about to croak. You know what kind of fights I've seen in front of the garbage bins? There's these two gals, a gypsy and maybe an Afghani fighting over a half-eaten sandwich. Talk about a brawl! So the gypsy gives her a whack like the whole thing was hers for the eating. This Muslim broad is bawling her head off and her face is all puffed up from the slaps. Just great, lady! I yell at her. Dirty beggars, the lot of 'em! That's why we're going to hit 'em where it hurts, in the stomach. Where they'll feel it."

What do you mean?

Now he's on a roll.

"Like mice, pal; like rats."

Meaning?

"Your family isn't from some village? How do you kill mice? You don't know?"

I stare at him. I want to show I'm running out of patience.

"Cement and water, pal, a little of each. What's it rats like? Cheese, like everybody knows. So you put little bowls here and there in your house. In one you put grated cheese mixed with quick-setting cement. So the rat comes and eats and since it's hungry and can never get enough and always in a rush it doesn't pay attention and stuffs it in. The other bowl you fill with water, the rat wants a drink and the water goes straight to its belly and turns into concrete and pop goes the rat. A natural extermination method, no chemicals, no nothing."

How's that related to what we're talking about? I ask him.

"Pal, you know what I'm talking about, you see it on TV. Screwdrivers, knives; fists, anything they can find. Busted heads, ribs, punctured lungs plus the odd corpse, one here, the other there. A few streets over, down the hill, in the back alleys; found two guys in the trash bins. Go on, tell me all about scavengers. The Paki opens the bin and he spots one of his own inside, let me tell you he won't do it again. A snapshot of his future is what he sees and he'll shit all over himself and he'll head straight for Islamabad or Nairobi or wherever the fuck he came from."

I go with the flow, just to get the journey over quicker. I ask him to explain what he means.

"You never heard about the porcelain bombs? About the blankets?"

No, never heard of bombs being made from something fragile like porcelain. Must have been another word game of his. With feigned patience I ask for details.

"The whites, pal, when they went to America, what did they do? To get rid of the Indians? Who were within their rights, we've got to be fair. So they give 'em blankets as charity handouts but the blankets are infected with smallpox, from the hospitals. A real epidemic. The Indians want blankets, they take 'em and even say thanks and down they go. One village after another. So the trick is, if you want to wipe 'em out, get 'em when they need it worst. If water don't work, get 'em with the food."

What's he going to say about porcelain? I ask, with real curiosity.

"The Japs, pal, the real masters. What do the Chinese eat? Rice is what they eat. So when the Japanese are fighting 'em they drop porcelain bowls full of rice from planes. Thousands. But the rice has fleas in it and the fleas have plague. Get it now?"

Not really.

"We take bread, add the poison, put it in a bag and hang it from the garbage bins like charitable souls, Paki takes it, down goes Paki. Got it now?"

The palms of my hands are sweating; carefully I wipe them on my trousers. Laugh as though he's joking. Turn my head and look at the other passengers. Maybe they didn't hear; he's not talking so loudly now.

Nobody will ever get wind of it? I ask him again.

"What's there to hear, pal? Some Afghan scavenger turns up dead from food poisoning? What else is he gonna die of, high cholesterol? Who even gives a shit? And tomorrow someone else, and then another few a few blocks over, and a family down the street. Just find me a journalist who'll report it, pal; a cop who'll ask questions. Some doctor who'll put two and two together. What are we, CSI Las Vegas? They'll never know what hit 'em I'm telling you, these people are sub-humans; they don't talk to each other. Just fight, like animals. Like I said, all kinds of races. Like they came, they'll leave. You'll never even notice."

The washbasin

WE PULLED A GOOD TWO SACKS OF CRABS from the creek that night, when the moon was full. After that, once we lit a fire and ate most of 'em there beside the spring, we threw the sacks over our shoulders and set off to steal Despo's washbasin, me and your uncle Panos, the practical joker; he liked to come along with me to catch crabs. We had our eye on that washbasin. It was a gift from her son-in-law in Tripoli. The guy who married her oldest girl. She kept it in the yard, sitting on a stump where the whole village could see it. Every morning they lined up to wash, her first and then her husband Karamitsos and then the kids. Mitso, she'd yell, the towel, Mitso, the water's heated. Come on, Mitso, get off your ass. Stuff like that. You could hear them all over the village. Then Despo would wash again. That's the way she was.

We snuck into her yard through the side gate, pulled it off the stump and made off with it, holding onto the wash basin one hand each and a sack of crabs the other. We didn't damage it though, made sure no one could tell it was us who took it; we were respectful kids; the thing was made of iron, cast iron for sure; it weighed a ton, and we hauled it up the hill, to the threshing floor. We hung it upside down on the stake in the middle they harnessed the mules to. We got there just before sun-up. Then we divided the crabs and headed home. We were—what?—fourteen or fifteen.

Wasn't long before all hell broke loose. I'd just managed to lie down and the ruckus started. The whole village was wide awake. Such howling you never heard. Everybody sticks their heads out the doors, the windows, the yards; some others who left already to mind the goats come to a stop; others turn back along the road, others just leave their animals alone with the dogs and rush off to see what's happened.

Thieves! Scoundrels, she howled. My washbasin. Her husband joined the chorus; shut your goddamned mouth woman, stop your yelling. You're making us look bad. We organized teams to look for the missing washbasin. Even Despo joined the search. I pretended to be looking hard, down the hillside in the other direction from where we hid the thing. The whole village, I'm telling you.

Plus people were curious; maybe they'd find it and get a close-up look at that famous washbasin everybody was talking about. Took 'em an hour. Who would have thought to look in the most obvious place. Everybody gathered around up at the threshing floor and stared. Like nobody had ever seen anything like it.

And so Despo got her washbasin back. The village talked about it for days. Who did it; who could it have been? Only my mom, your grandmother, figured it out right away. You did it George, she said. With put-on anger, wagging her finger at me. Despo never washed her face in the yard again. She moved the washbasin inside and there it stayed.

Later Karamitsos, who was my father's first cousin, one day when they were reminiscing about the past, just last year in fact, told him that when they were taking the washtub back to the house what should jump out but a crab. And that nobody else in the village went crabbing except George. Me, that is!

Soon after I left. Came up to Athens in sixty-two. Nope, sixty-three. Lived in Vathis Square, in a room I rented from an old lady. The old bag would bring me fruit, a watermelon now and then. An apple. Just gave it to me. I had an electric fan I never told her about. So I wouldn't have to pay more for electricity. I lock the door, pull it out of my suitcase and turn it on, to get a cool breeze. One night the fan breaks down; the old lady catches on. All I had to my name back then was a knife. And a bedroll. Finally, when the room began to really stink I slung the bedroll over my shoulder and stuck the knife in my pocket and took off. Before I met your mom I lived in a good twenty different rooms. From sixty-three to seventy-four. Twenty different rooms, twenty different streets. Pankrati was where I was living when I met your mom.

Got my first job in the square at Vic City. Sure there was work back then, but what kind of work? Snack bars; pastry shops. Put out the chairs and tables; move 'em back in. The owner, from Mani he was, a good man, says be here at eight o'clock. So next day I show up he hands me a glass of hot milk to drink and hands me a broom. Take it and clean the square. For a half-hour, an hour I'm sweeping, the passers-by are staring at me. Hard work doesn't scare me, you know. But the square's big, and I'm embarrassed there in the middle of all those people. So this is your Athens, I say to myself. I leave the broom in a corner, go into the shop, how much do I owe for the milk boss I'm leaving, I tell him. I came up to Athens to find better. Not to clean up everybody else's mess. If that's how things are I would have stayed in the village and gathered cow pats. Better village cow pats than Athenian shit, I said.

＊ ＊ ＊

I ask him, surprised by my investigative skills, what happens if some Greek eats it.

"We've got it covered. Whoever puts out the sack of bread has to wait. You hide out somewhere close. If he looks to you like one of us, you go and distract him or you buy him a loaf of bread so he won't have to eat garbage."

He notices my surprise.

"Your mouth's wide open. Let me tell you, it's like modern cockroach poison; you know how it works? The roach takes some, carries it back to its nest and before long they're all dead. Just remember what I said."

He stops; winks at me. I hope he's joking. The light is starting to fade; we can't be too far from Athens. I want to change the subject. I tell him I don't think there's any such thing as Vic City, to the best of my knowledge.

I ask him for confirmation.

"What do you mean, pal?"

The place, I say, the place called Vic City, not Victoria Square or just the subway station, right? I ask in as friendly a way as I can, regretting I ever asked him in the first place. Suddenly he leans toward me.

"And me, where do I live, pal? What have I been telling you all this time?"

I worked for a legal firm, I tell him, tracking down property titles. Never once saw "Victoria" written anywhere. Written down, you know; on a document. Kypseli I've seen, for example. My idea is that "Victoria" is part of Kypseli. And if you say "I live in Victoria" that really only means the people who live right on the square and all the rest, strictly speaking of course, live in the Kypseli district, which is a lot bigger. Or maybe in Patissia? Strictly speaking, I mean.

He waves his hand back and forth.

"Are you in your right mind pal? Victoria exists and then some! What's this Kypseli bullshit? Victoria! Vic City like we call it! Guys like us, we grew up there and that's where we live. Kids from Kypseli, we'd beat the piss out of 'em buddy; they wouldn't dare show their faces. What Patissia are you talking about anyway? No such place, you say; what a pile of crap. So what does that make me, buddy? Where did I grow up? St. Paraskevi exists but not Vic City? I grew up in nowhere? Pal, you're full of it. Really full of it, and that's a shame!"

He smacks the arm rest with his hand. I look around for an empty seat. None to be seen. All you can hear is the click-click of the rails. When everybody pretends not to notice you, that's exactly when you're the only one they're looking at. I really need to get some sleep. There he is, right across from me, pursing his lips until they've become a thin white line, and staring straight at me.

I don't turn away; simply close my eyes. My heart is beating faster now, and for an instant I almost expect him to hit me. I sit there, eyes closed. Absolutely nothing happens.

I wake up when we arrive. My traveling companion is no longer seated across from me.

Incubator

WE'RE TALKING ABOUT PATISSIA STREET back
when it was still a dirt road, way back when.
I just had Voula, my fourth daughter; Vlassis
couldn't get over it, not having a son, but he
didn't let on, not right away at any rate. And
she was just a tiny thing, no more than three
pounds. She needs an incubator says the doctor, what's that doctor? I say, a machine he
says, how much does it cost doctor, I can't
remember, ten thousand drachmas he says,
maybe fifteen he says. I don't have that kind

of money I say, what can we do? So I twist his arm and he tells me how to do it and I make the incubator myself. Yep. With milk bottles, they were glass back then. I bought another gas burner just in case the first one broke down and I'm stuck without gas day and night I boiled water, filled the bottles, wrapped them in blankets and put them in her cradle, all around. The doc loaned me a thermometer I don't remember what temperature it shouldn't go below. Forty degrees, that's what it was. Every two hours I changed the bottles. Nobody could come into the room. Only me. For the germs and for quiet. Nothing to upset her. The whole thing went on for three months. And I did it; a pink-cheeked kid. As pink as a rosebud. When the doctor saw her he couldn't believe his eyes. "Do it," is what he told me, "and whatever God wills will happen." I don't know if it was God's will. But it was my will for sure.

Meanwhile Vlassis left. Cleared out. Good riddance. People started to talk. Somebody saw him on the BMW, that crappy motorbike of his, speeding down by the seashore at Skaramangka, where the shipyards are. Later someone spotted him in Salonica. That blabbermouth Elpiniki who lives just across the hall found out everything. He was up north with another woman. Plus two kids. Later someone spotted him near St. Panteleimon's. I asked questions. I wasn't ashamed of nothing. Then he moved, along with her, two streets down from our house, can you imagine? He was making money and she was spending it all. So every day I sent one of the girls across from his place, to find out what he was doing. Mostly Gogo, my oldest, who wasn't working yet plus she always did what I told her. She stood there and waited. For hours. Don't you budge from there or else; you come back home at night and tell me everything. And she saw her dad going in and out, sometimes by himself, sometimes with her or with those other kids of his. And she came and told me everything. Me, I grilled her. Maybe you talked to him, kid, I said. Maybe you crossed the street and talked to him? Maybe he saw you? No, she said. "Who are those kids anyway?" she asked. Don't ask I told her; your father knows. But she had it figured out and kept her mouth shut. She was no fool. Not one lousy drachma, not one lousy phone call for two years, the bum. A marriage and four kids, written on the sand, all of it.

No telling what I would have done without blind Tassos, the best man at our wedding. He did what he could to help out. He'd bring some clothes, something for us to eat, money the odd time, or a box of sweets. Vlassis's friend. A good man. He felt sorry for me, but he never had a bad word to say about his chum. Even when he was a kid he liked reading but they wouldn't let him. His folks had some animals, a few sheep and his job was to mind them, somewhere not far from town. But he kept on buying books and magazines, whatever he could find and hid out in the trees so he could read. That's how he was. All the time reading. Didn't want to lose his place. One time he was so distracted the animals got away. His father comes looking for him and the animals are missing and after awhile he spots him there in a mulberry tree reading. Hadn't even noticed; just a kid. So his father throws a rock at him and it hits him smack in the eye. They took it out. Bit by bit he started having trouble seeing out of the other eye. It just went dry. He ended up blind. The Welfare gave him a stall in front of the Athens city hall, and he earned a wage. Selling straw sandals.

But Vlassis, he finally comes back, back to the little nest that nobody but him had fouled. And the other woman shows up out-side the house and yells "hey, you cheap whore, give me my man back." You heard what I said: 'her man!' Once he brings me a chicken, the greedy pig, could never get enough to eat the guy, "cook it with butter" he tells me. I ignore him. For a chicken so fat you could get three pots of soup out of it I was going to waste butter? So we sit down to eat and he says how come you didn't cook it with butter like I told you and he starts to cuss me out and then some, I say listen buddy you want me to cook this thing with butter, you're damned right you dumb shit broad. Me, that's it. I'm furious. So I take the soup bowl and whack I smack him with it, right on top of his head. Hair full of carrots and celery. Good job the girls are there; they save me. He grabs a chair to hit me but they give him a shove and he drops it. Sure, he whacks me more than a couple of times, he really lays into me but not with the chair. He'd have killed me. He only stops when he hears 'daddy, daddy' and turns around and sees the whole neighborhood right there in our front yard, on Filis Street it was. Front and center is Elpiniki. They're all staring at him, nobody saying a thing. Only then he drops the belt. What are you staring at he says, get out of my house. Then he picks up the chicken from the ground, shakes it off as best he can, sets the chair back on four legs and starts to wolf it down.

* * *

I come out of the railway station and into the crowd of people rushing by. My legs feel numb after so many hours sitting down. My head the same. I put down my travel bag and light a cigarette. At last; the nicotine calms me. Already everything I heard for so many hours on the train seems like it never happened. Like it was all a dream. Pushed into the background by the press of reality. Real reality. People coming and going, exhaust fumes, noise. It's chilly. I take a few more drags.

A black woman wearing a black dress and a black headscarf runs into me. She's carrying a baby marsupial style and holding another by the hand. Walking fast. Looks healthy; life can't be too bad. A bit on the plump side, even. She's in no danger, I say to myself. Doesn't look like the kind of person who would eat garbage. I push the ridiculous thought from my mind and rub out the cigarette on the sidewalk. Right in front of me walks a guy in rags pushing a cart full of scrap metal, wire, a radiator, and rusted hubcaps. A gypsy woman comes up to me. Hey good looking, got a cigarette? Tell your fortune? I give her a cigarette, pick up my bag and step sideways to get away from her. She grabs my arm. Not so fast, let me tell your fortune. I pull my arm away and move on. I run into two gypsy kids—hers?—and almost step on them; they're shaking a plastic cup with small change. Without a word they hold it out to me, they don't believe I'll give them something. And go on with their game; something like hopscotch. I step around them and head for the barrier that separates the sidewalk from the street, moving rapidly toward the opening that leads to the other side. I feel a growing sense of anxiety. I reach the spot, at the pedestrian signal light. In front of me is a family from the provinces, each member carrying plaid bags. Beside me, an elderly man is bent over a garbage bin, rummaging through the waste paper and bottles barehanded. White hair; white beard. Greek? Don't do it, I almost tell him; be careful, but I don't spot any bag hanging there. The light turns green and I hurry across until I reach the road divider where some taxis are lined up. I head for the lead car. Not much space; only one pedestrian at a time. My travel bag is weighing me down. Toward me comes a young guy, probably an Arab, wearing a leather jacket. Instinctively I step aside and into the street on my right. I hear a horn and a scooter loaded with huge plastic bags where the driver's legs should be rushes by. Some Asian probably. I jump back onto the pedestrian platform with a mix of fear and irritation. Just a couple more taxis and finally I'll reach the head of the line. Right in front of me is a bench, for people waiting for a car I reason. On it a fat, bearded bare-footed man is sleeping blissfully. Next to the first taxi a group of drivers are laughing and shouting. I dump my bag in the trunk and shut it hard, on purpose. They turn around and look at me, and one of them steps out of the group and gets into the driver's seat.

As I reach for the door handle I feel a hand grab the back of my neck. So hard I bite my tongue.

"Say, pal! Not even a fare-thee-well? That's how you sneak out? Anyway, off you go. And if you're in the area, you can look me up: Vic City. If you can find it that is."

He winks, releases his grip, slaps me again on the back and walks off at a brisk pace. As I step into the cab my cell pings. More emails. The first spams of the new day. | Unlimited gym access | Beat cellulite | 4-hand massage | Kokkoni vacation village | Should I tell Vasso? She's been talking about a vacation. Ping, I forward the message. She'll be happy. Plus I'll butter her up a bit. Things haven't been right between us for a while now. Never heard of Kokkoni; I could use a vacation too, no doubt about it.

I give the driver my destination. Immediately I regret what I just did: what if Vasso, who's not really on my side these days, on account of things aren't all that great between us, thinks I didn't forward that email because of the Kokkoni holiday but on account of the cellulite treatment? On account of the cellulite that's shown up lately in a curious place, behind her thighs. No way I couldn't notice it. I remember the repulsion I felt at that tiny sign of physical decay. As we drove off I noticed out of the corner of my eye that the fat guy on the bench had awakened, sat up, put his bare feet on the pavement and was holding his head in his hands. Exactly the way I wake up every morning.

I pick up the cell to call my wife; please turn down the radio I ask the driver.

It's Monday morning and the sports commentators are analyzing yesterday's games at the top of their lungs.

Afterword by Fred A. Reed

STRICTLY SPEAKING A COLLECTION of short stories—interlocking variations on a theme of acute social distress—*Vic City Express* introduces English-speaking readers to a Greece that they are unlikely to ever encounter. A Greece catastrophically impacted by the flood tides of globalization and the concomitant destruction of what once was once a deeply traditional society.

Yannis Tsirbas locates his account in Vic City, which the book's anonymous narrator insists does not exist. It does indeed exist, argues the talkative and threatening protagonist on the train to Athens: the very real district in south-central Athens centered on the Victoria metro station. Once a lively working-class neighbourhood not far from the former site of the Athens Polytechnic where student demonstrators began the movement that brought down the country's fascist junta in 1974, Vic City is now populated largely by immigrants and refugees that Greece, wracked by depression, cannot hope to integrate into its failing social network.

Hovering over *Vic City Express* is the shadow of Hryssi Avgi—Golden Dawn—the virulent Greek neo-fascist movement. From its origins as a marginal post-junta extreme nationalist party, Golden Dawn was able to leverage the Greek debt crisis to emerge as the country's third-ranking political party, with 17 deputies in the Greek National Assembly.

The party's youth wing has organized "attack squadrons" that operate in those parts of Greece's major cities hardest hit by the crisis that has left more than 25 percent of the population unemployed. Its tactics include the distribution of food to "racially pure" Greeks unable to make ends meet and the systematic intimidation of immigrants—including beatings and public threats, and sometimes murder.

Golden Dawn was given new impetus by the arrival from Turkey on Greece's Aegean islands of tens of thousands of refugees from the conflicts raging in the Middle East in the wake of the United States' 2003 invasion of Iraq and its subsequent efforts to topple the government of Syrian president Bashar al-Assad.

Efforts in Greece to curb the party's influence have been relatively unsuccessful, despite its being labeled a "criminal organization" with demonstrable links to Nazi ideological sources. Greece's police forces, known for their close collaboration with the 1967-1974 junta, are today suspected of sympathy for Golden Dawn's program.

Just as there is no beauty in Vic City, there is little but raw brutality in author Tsirbas's language. This raw brutality is on display particularly in the sequence involving Meleti, the punk who ends up emasculated by the police, and who may well be the immigrant-killer protagonist encountered on the train to Athens.

Readers might well wonder why the youth's decision to have "police" tattooed on his penis so enrages that very police. In Modern Greek street language, one 'writes' the name of someone he wishes to insult or demean on one's genitals. Taken seriously, it is a grave insult designed to attack and destroy the self-esteem—the *filotimo*—of the person so demeaned. Meleti, in tattooing the word 'police' on his virile member has crossed the line, laid down a life-or-death challenge to the enforcers of authority.

Maps of Athens show the Victoria metro station and the warren of narrow streets that surround it: Vic City. What they do not show is the hunger, despair and destitution that has destroyed the social fabric; what they do not show is the massive influx of refugees and immigrants that Greek society has manifestly been unable to assimilate.

The immense merit of *Vic City Express* is that it shines full and merciless light on a society in distress, and on the social and economic crisis that has given birth to a monster.

Fred A. Reed, Outremont, July 2018

Printed by Imprimerie Gauvin
Gatineau, Québec